THIS BOOK IS PRESENTED TO

____

ON THIS DAY

____

FROM

____

THE TWELVE DAYS OF CHRISTMAS

DAN ANDREASEN

PUBLISHED BY SLEEPING BEAR PRESS

Sleeping Bear Press™
315 East Eisenhower Parkway, Suite 200
Ann Arbor, MI 48108
www.sleepingbearpress.com

Printed and bound in the United States.

10 9 8 7 6 5 4 3 2 1

Library of Congress Cataloging-in-Publication Data
Twelve days of Christmas (English folk song)
The twelve days of Christmas / illustrated by Dan Andreasen.
p. cm.
Summary: Presents the words to the traditional song of gifts given on each of the twelve days of Christmas, with illustrations of French hens wearing berets, loud calling birds, and more.
ISBN 978-1-58536-834-1 (hardback)
1. Folk songs, English--England--Texts. 2. Christmas music--Texts.
[1. Folk songs--England. 2. Christmas music.] I. Title.
PZ8.3.T8517 2012
782.42--dc23
[E]
2012007623

For Sharon

—Dan

On the first day of Christmas
My true love gave to me
A partridge in a pear tree.

On the second day of Christmas
My true love gave to me
Two turtle doves and
A partridge in a pear tree.

On the third day of Christmas
My true love gave to me
Three French hens
Two turtle doves and
A partridge in a pear tree.

On the fourth day of Christmas
My true love gave to me
Four calling birds
Three French hens
Two turtle doves and
A partridge in a pear tree.

On the fifth day of Christmas
My true love gave to me
Five golden rings
Four calling birds
Three French hens
Two turtle doves and
A partridge in a pear tree.

On the sixth day of Christmas
My true love gave to me
Six geese a-laying
Five golden rings
Four calling birds
Three French hens
Two turtle doves and
A partridge in a pear tree.

On the seventh day of Christmas
My true love gave to me
Seven swans a-swimming
Six geese a-laying
Five golden rings
Four calling birds
Three French hens
Two turtle doves and
A partridge in a pear tree.

On the eighth day of Christmas
My true love gave to me
Eight maids a-milking
Seven swans a-swimming
Six geese a-laying

Five golden rings
Four calling birds
Three French hens
Two turtle doves and
A partridge in a pear tree.

On the ninth day of Christmas
My true love gave to me
Nine ladies dancing
Eight maids a-milking
Seven swans a-swimming
Six geese a-laying
Five golden rings
Four calling birds
Three French hens
Two turtle doves and
A partridge in a pear tree.

On the tenth day of Christmas
My true love gave to me
Ten lords a-leaping
Nine ladies dancing
Eight maids a-milking

Seven swans a-swimming
Six geese a-laying
Five golden rings
Four calling birds
Three French hens
Two turtle doves and
A partridge in a pear tree.

On the eleventh day of Christmas
My true love gave to me
Eleven pipers piping
Ten lords a-leaping
Nine ladies dancing
Eight maids a-milking
Seven swans a-swimming
Six geese a-laying
Five golden rings
Four calling birds
Three French hens
Two turtle doves and
A partridge in a pear tree.

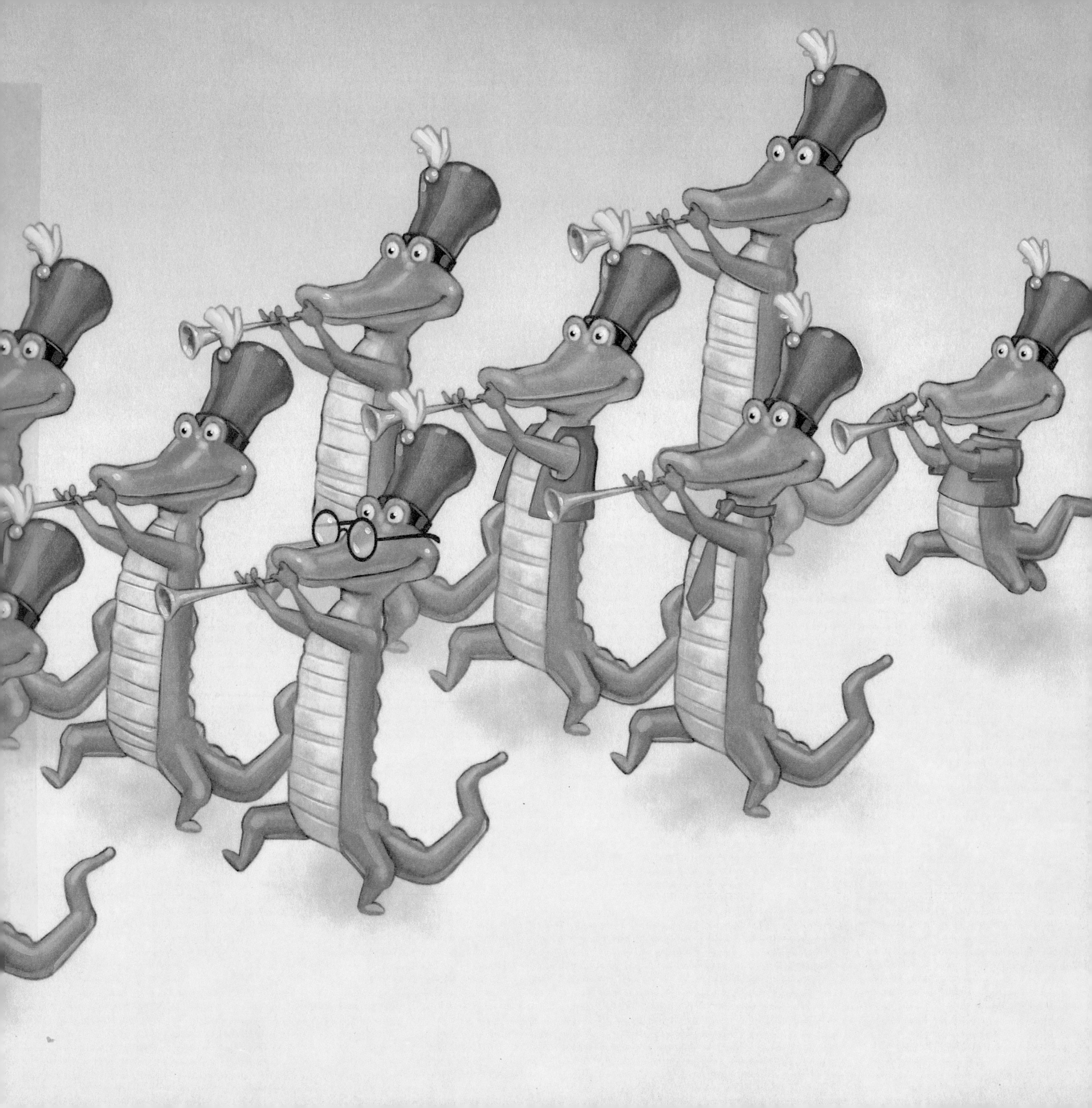

On the twelfth day of Christmas
My true love gave to me
Twelve drummers drumming
Eleven pipers piping
Ten lords a-leaping
Nine ladies dancing
Eight maids a-milking
Seven swans a-swimming
Six geese a-laying
Five golden rings
Four calling birds
Three French hens
Two turtle doves and
A partridge
in a pear tree.